DAN AND GRAMPS

Jean Watson

Illustrated by Toni Goffe

VICTOR BOOKS

A DIVISION OF SCRIPTURE PRESS PUBLICATIONS INC.
USA CANADA ENGLAND

Dan and his great-granddad lived near each other. Dan called him Gramps.

Dan often came around to see Gramps. If he came about 11 o'clock in the morning, they had drinks and biscuits, which Gramps called "elevenses." If he came at about 4 o'clock in the afternoon, they had drinks and cake, which Dan called "fourses."

Gramps was good at losing things and Dan was good at finding them.

One day Dan brought his new storybook to Gramps. But Gramps had lost his reading glasses. Dan had to look everywhere before he found them. It was wonderful.

"Well I never!" said Gramps when he saw them too. He put them on and read the new storybook to Dan.

Another day Gramps lost his walking stick. Dan couldn't find it anywhere in the house. But he soon saw where it was trying to hide in the back garden.

"Bless my soul!" said Gramps. Then he took his walking stick and Dan to the store and bought Dan an ice cream cone.

Then Gramps broke his false teeth.

"I know I had a shpare shet shomewhere," he said. When Dan had worked out what he meant, he went and hunted for Gramps' spare set. He found it, eventually. Gramps couldn't understand how they'd got there but he gave them a good cleaning, then put them in.

"That's better," he said. "Now we can each have an apple."

On another day Gramps lost a slipper. Dan couldn't see it anywhere at first. Then he burst out laughing and said, "Look, Gramps."

"Oh well," said Gramps when he saw what Dan was pointing at. "I don't really need it. Not for the moment anyway."

Then Gramps lost his hat. Dan looked in all the usual places. But it wasn't in any of those. So he started looking in all the unusual places and found it in one of those.

When Gramps saw where it was, he said, "Fancy that!" and put the hat cozily on his head. Then he and Dan went to the park with some "eating bread" for themselves and some "duck bread" for the ducks.

One Sunday in church, Gramps lost his offering money.

After the service, the whole family hunted for it. But they couldn't find it.

"It'll turn up," said Gramps.

And it did, when Dan handed Gramps his gloves.

"I *knew* I'd put my money in a safe place," said Gramps. Dan took it to the people who were counting the offering money.

Afterward, they went to Dan's house and
enjoyed one of Mom's famous Sunday lunches.

Then Dan and Dad walked Gramps back to his house for a rest.

When they reached the front door, Gramps exclaimed, "Oh dear! My key! It must still be in church."

"No, it's not!" said Dan with a smile. "I put it in a safe place for you." And he took it out of his pocket and held it up.

"Me and my forgettory!" said Gramps, taking the key and opening the door. "Good thing God takes care of me!"

"God?" exclaimed Dan, rather surprised and a little annoyed.

"Yes," said Gramps. "By giving me a kind family and good friends. Especially my very helpful great-grandson."

Dan smiled. It was nice being called helpful. It gave him a warm and tickly feeling inside.

1 2 3 4 5 6 7 8 9 10 Printing/Year 99 98 97 96 95

© 1995 Scripture Union. All rights reserved.
Text © 1995, Jean Watson
Illustrations © 1995, Toni Goffe

Published in the United States by Victor Books / SP Publications Inc.,
Wheaton, Illinois.
Printed in Singapore.

ISBN: 1-56476-364-1